MW01127907

AND WE ALL BREATHE THE SAME AIR

www.augiesbookshelf.com

HEATH
ROBINSON

AND WE ALL BREATHE THE SAME AIR

AND WE ALL BREATHE THE SAME AIR

Published by: Augie's Bookshelf

Text Design by: Molly Wolchansky

Cover Artwork by: Sean Cairns

Cover Design by: Brady Wolchansky

A CIP record for this book is available from the Library of Congress Cataloging-in-Publication Data

Printed and bound in The United States

ISBN 9781796973549

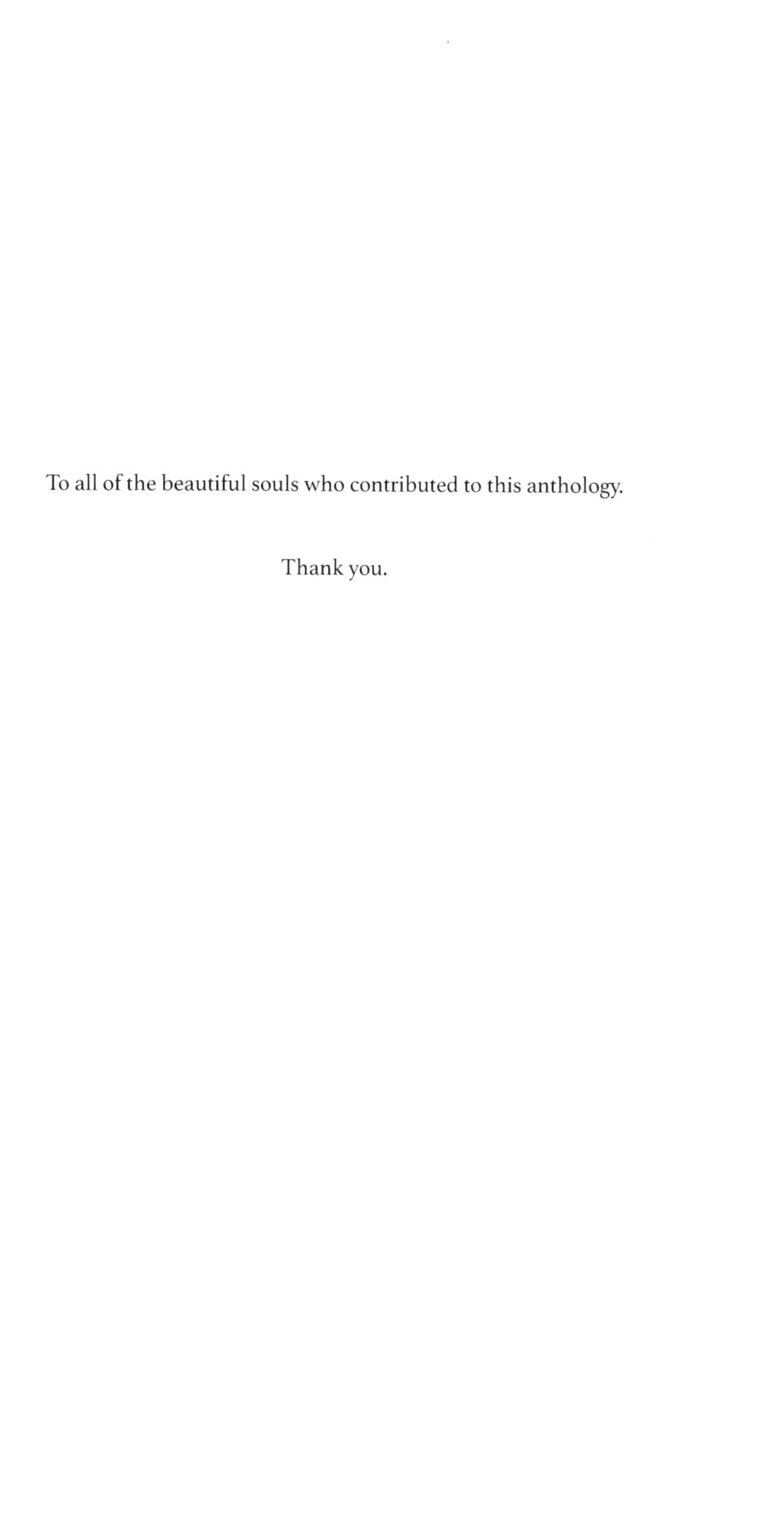

To all of the beautiful souls who contributed to this anthology.

Thank you.

Contents

Clothos.

You doodled on my arm

Out of boredom—

A random, meaningless pattern

With a cheap, fading pen.

But to me,

It was gorgeous

Because it was your design,

Conceived from your endlessly

Complex and innovative mind.

For a moment,

I wanted it tattooed

Onto my skin

So that your artistry

Would be captured,

And I'd forever be your canvas

Because of one small moment

Of childish intimacy.

86

-c.k.c

@ckayclark

We sat on the sofa

By the window

I smoked a cigarette

And so did he

He was a hypocrite

Asked me when I'd quit

As he dragged on

His foreign Marlboro

A playlist floated

From a makeshift speaker

"It works the same"

He said

As he put my phone

In a glass

And let me

Choose the songs

He showed me one or two

I listen to them when

I miss him

-Sian Marie

@sianmariepoetry

Mouth pressed above my brow,
Arms around my waist,
I move my mouth to meet your face,
You lean away,
I embrace the chase,
I close my eyes in anticipation of you reigning down on me,
Your kisses remind me of feathers,
Gently falling slowly,
Your nimble fingers caress my back,
In this I have all faith,
Like two feathers dancing on silk sheets,
That's the love we make.

Feathers
-Bettie Schade
@bettie_schade

I have gone through far too much thunder
To let my body be diminished by society's standards.

My body is a plant which blossoms daily:
It will grow from light and watering,
It will not submit to storms and violent wind.

It will stand tall and take in what nourishes it,
It will absorb the sunshine and root itself
Deeper into its own strength and acceptance,
It will love and be loved by its own leaves and branches
And it will be proud to carry itself so fearlessly
That nothing will ever get in the way of its
Beautiful, healthy and natural growth.

Self-Love

-Noemie Del Duca

@ndelducapoetry

I hope you find love. I hope you find a love that would set your soul at peace, a love that would ease your nervous laughs and trembling fingers. I hope you find a love that would free you from your own perception of who you need to be, from the illusion of a stereotype that you need to fit into to be worthy of love.
I hope you find a love that would make you comprehend that the world doesn't revolve around you. I hope you fall in love that would leave you only a truer version of yourself.
I hope you find home in someone's heart.

Love

-Basma Eletreby

@basma.etreby

It has been
a while
since someone
has tread
these vacant floors.

My fingers
trace scars
on barren walls
wounds
from
torn down portraits
of past lovers.

It has been
a while
since the
window shutters
breathed.
Could sunlight
pierce
this heavy dust
thick with
the odor of
broken promises?

I open them.

Witness
the marigold sun
rise
on the horizon.

The petals
from
its garland
flutter
into every
crevice
destitute
of affection.

As I dance
to each inhale
and exhale,
lighting incense
in every chamber.
My footsteps
sweep away
the dust.

I climb your fears
to decorate
the entryway
with daffodils.

The void
once entombed
in darkness,
where
you only heard
the quiet cries
of lonely air,
echoes with my
laughter.
Floorboards groan
with pleasure
touched
by a lover
after
so long.
In the
hollows
of your heart
I have
made
my home.

Hollows of Your Heart
- Harpreet M. Dayal
@harpreet.m.dayal

We are so much alike. People like us are rare,
hard to find and hard to lose.
We love with every breath in our bones
and in between the beats of our hearts.
We go to the ends of the earth to provide peace
for the ones we love the most.
We give and give and give some more,
and most of the time don't know when to stop.
Because it's who we are. It's burned in our blood.
That's why we tend to be broken more often.
We never learn what we learn,
Because we just do it all over again.
For the sake of love, and for the notion
that we ourselves are greater than
broken hearts and shattered dreams.

Humans like us;

-Kayil York

@rose_thorns1921

Hearts

have a funny

way of healing,

bit by bit

by

b

i

t

-Perry Poetry

@perrypoetry

in that moment, as you
looked at me, all
other thoughts
vanished: i was
ecstatic, secretly
yielding to this new
outrageous truth: an
unconditional love for you

an acrostic confession
-Scott-Patrick Mitchell
@spmpoet

The Book

I wanted to write

a book

about Us

but how could I

when

Our ending

is only in

Chapter One?

a very short love story

-Marsha A.

@poetistpanda

ease my hunger
in the aperture
of your eye
using my shadow
and your light
capture the ceremony
of my skin
unearth my fire
in swells and rolls
undulating the edges
of my heart
dissolving all apology
wring the sponge dry
and leave me
anticipating you

undulations
-Jenn Dessert
@quiet.little.mercies

You see me
in the overcrowded market,
pass colorful linen
that shakes the fragrance of dahlias
through hot moist air,
near fresh guavas
dripping for attention.

You come here every week,
adorned with precious garments
and gems,
to seek out treasure.

The others say
that I am not pretty enough for you;
that I am ugly.
But I heard that true beauty lies inside
like a fruit
beneath its outer layer,
which may be scratched or bruised.
It is the sweet taste
of its nourishment
that truly matters,
so I am told.

Love in the Marketplace
-Marc Bayard
@bayard.marc

years later
and there are still poems
blooming
inbetween your breaths.

-Abigail Zerr
@rainbow_ink

Like spills that tarnished lacquered wood
You stained my soul in rims
With every coffee cup that stood
And grew cold upon the window sill
As we read and talked and wrote
And danced
Deep into the darkness
That pink wall bled its honesty
And hid us from the world
And it asked for nothing in return
But silence and the written word

We sat upon the soft warm floor
And broke a thousand times together
But the cracks, they didn't matter
They only made me love you more

And then the storm came lashing in
And the old tall house could hold no sin
It shook with Rage and whipped the curtain
with no sound,
pretending
pretending to be Gentle

And I have been back there since

To visit the Us that was

But they milked it white

And tried to clean the memories –

Only sunlight streams in now

Marking shadows from the window panes

In check blocks of right and wrong.

No matter now

I stain my fingers on these strings

Remembering

Remembering you in everything

Of Pink Walls and Rememberings

-Ghabiba Weston

@ghabibaweston

*

It's been a minute

Stacks of 60 seconds

All rolled up in days

Categorized by months

Stretched into years.

And with each year

A mixed bag of emotional seasons

Embraced by arms, laced around my body.

Arms that hold strength of fathers

That were and are to come.

With a touch as gentle as a whisper

Of sweet melodies and promises.

I say this unto you:

As a reminder.

As a lover.

As a thank you.

That I will

Gladly take

Every spare 60 seconds

And invest it in more years with you.

60 Second Love

-Jesselyne Abel

@ink.jess

and darling

as the moon changed

so did our love.

some days

i was full

of

hope and

compassion

and stardust.

while others

i was dry out

of everything

needed

to keep us

together.

but the thing about the moon

darling,

is that it's always changing,

and you,

were always there

through every phase.

Moon Dance

-Grace

@fairly.grace

I want to bury myself in you
Then you bury yourself into me
We'll evaporate through fusion
Atoms, molecules out into the space
We will flame from the sun
frost from the dark night
And flux into a star light
We will travel in our milky way
Land on an earth far from this earth
With green oceans and blue trees
Create our own species
We'll make rabbits for dragons
Birds for butterflies
Flowers as big as mountains,
I dream of us out of my senses
and you bring me back to my essence.

-Adem Osman
@acrookedpoet

I handed you my heart

I knew we were right
for each other
when you handed me yours

and it was just as full
just as heavy
as my own.

-Samantha Gray
@s.l._gray

By chance

If my good karma is just

Getting to be in your presence

If my stars happen to be

The ones I see in your eyes

If destiny is real and

We happen to share one

Then I'll love you as if

Stepping on a crack

Evil eyes and

Black cats

Can decide our fate

Because these superstitions

May match my paranoia

But desire and effort together

Are larger than the supernatural

Don't Let the Unknown Scare You

- M. Maan

@mmaanpoetry

She unfolds me like a piece of paper
on which she has scribbled her soul
in sensual verse
that feels practiced but not rehearsed
and when she has had her fill
she folds me up again
and places me in her pocket for later.

In the Folds of Her Love
-Ron Barton
@teacher2poet

there is something
about you
that makes me
fall for you
something in
the way you smile
that makes my spine
tingle
something about
your eyes
that makes my heart
melt
something in
the sound of your voice
that makes my knees
go weak
there is something
in you
that makes my mind
lose its sanity

Something About You
-Marsha A.
@poetistpanda

my naked body

is a work of art

I don't know

if the artist was

Rubens or Dali

or Picasso

I am trying

to find beauty

in it but isn't all

art subjective?

My Naked Body

-Isabella Mansfield

@isabellajmansfield

if lips can brush stories

onto our bones

the same way

artists

paint canvases

then keep one thought in mind:

stories are only true

if both bodies are listening.

-Abigail Zerr

@rainbow_ink

You are not alone
Multitudes of women have pondered
this
Spending precious years
in front of a mirror
pulling, poking, prodding
Staining our hair, eyes, lips, and skin
Silently begging for that one person to notice

Yet, our souls are razed
with each pluck and push
we shift our focus away from the truth.
The chant of a continual drum
beating out our movements
pretty
pretty
You see, my dears
pretty is a distraction
we imprint on innocent minds
too young to know better.

-Ashley Victoria
@Ashley.victoria.poetry

I peeled an orange
This Monday morning
And let its citrus fill my living room
I washed the dishes
And tidied the floors
Warmed up some soup
And opened a book
Threw on some background music
And wrapped myself in a sweater
Outside there's street noise
And a gentle breeze that reminds me
To once in a while glance out the window
and appreciate nature
It is a perfectly ordinary Monday morning
In this solitary, one-bedroom apartment
And I want nothing else, nothing more
Not even you, though my heart holds you close
No, I want nothing else, nothing more
For I know
How extraordinary it is
To have an ordinary morning
Feeling content at home.

A Morning

-t.s. ink

@inkskratches

We crunch the gravel
side by side
beneath our worn out shoes
The path is never lonely when
I am here with you
The dust it clouds on up like mist
to grate beneath our eyelids
And we forget to listen to the world
But it never stops your laughter
singing through the still night air
Maybe you don't mean to
but you keep the ghosts at bay
hidden in smudged crimson clouds,
mirrored in puddles of smooth red
clay
Our passage is dim with light
enough
to see what's just ahead
but I am not afraid
of darkness
and the sound of a forest black

You have found another road
I watch the light bounce off
your
back
It's so still now
that I have stopped a moment
And I can breathe again.
But I still hear your laughter
It floats my Spirit high
And for the first time,
I looked up
And saw Yours soaring in the
sky

The Road
-Ghabiba Weston
@ghabibaweston

Sun reflecting on ocean waves
Freckles and far away places
Fresh mountain air stargazing
Exploring forests evergreen
Blue eyes as calm as waterfalls
Raspberry sunsets over new snow
Stepping out of comfort zones
All of this and coming home.

What is Your Love Made Of?
-Sarah Herrin
@_sarahherrin

I have a love

Or lack thereof

Of the person before me.

I stare at my coffee colored eyes,

An entrance to all emotions and my soul.

I stare at my full lips,

A pathway for words to be music to one's ear.

I stare at my deep copper toned skin,

A beauty so bright it's imitated by others.

I have a love

Or lack thereof

Of the person before me.

I stare at my scars,

Healed wounds that are simply reminders of my failures.

Stare at my mistakes, short comings, empty promises.

I stare,

Even though mama says not to.

I stare.

I stare,

In love with the person before me.

With everything she lacks

With everything she has

For she is beauty in the eyes of her Maker.

One's Stare

-Jesselyne Abel

@ink.jess

you hide your thoughts

your feelings

your mind

from everyone

you keep it all to yourself

keep it mysterious and aloof

I think

that's a shame

because I'd

love to know

what's going on

in that head of yours

(speak your heart)

it's important

-Pia Rabea Linden

@rabearaphael

Morning whispers,
legs entwined,
the tickle of your skin in the soft light
that traces softly through these sheets.
you touch the places I never knew existed,
and I've never been happier
in this place,
with you, with me,
with us.

-Perry Poetry
@perrypoetry

As sunrise sketches a fresh piece of art
She hears a new melody from the depths of her heart
The tips of his fingers caress her heartstrings
The beat of his own she feels pulsing within
She wistfully hums this tune all the day long
With guitar now in hand she whispers
"I will write you a song"

Your Song

- Anne Joseph

@_annie_jo_

i can drape you
in the finest adjectives,
the most flattering metaphors.
(i admit, my love,
embellishment and exaggeration
look exquisite on you.)
i can disguise all
your least favorite qualities
with time-tested clichés
until you are nothing short
of poetic.
but do not forget
that even without any of it
you are nothing short
of poetic.
remember that at the end of the day,
you will still have to face yourself
unadorned. naked. raw.
(and i promise,
there is infinite beauty
in your natural.)
so, darling, please
take the time
to learn
to love yourself
that way.

natural
-Emily May Portillo
@poetry.on.the.exhale

Maneuvering through landmines
sailing through an ocean dark with storms
diving into waters infested with ravenous sharks
you say that's the danger you feel with me
Smelling a flower that'll be wilted by frost
listening to music that's long past its peak
hearing a child laugh, knowing they'll grow up
you say that's the melancholy you feel with me
Receiving an unexpected gift, wrapped in gold paper
making someone's day, watching the smile curl up
singing softly to the agitated, silencing their woes
you say that's the generosity you feel with me
So feel with me for eternity
we have a full palette of emotions
to paint with
by the time we're done
we'll have created a masterpiece
for the world to revere forevermore

Masterpiece

-Olwen Daisy

@olwendaisy_poetry

Love her when she can't stand on her own two feet.
Even though she says she's ok, wrap your arms
around her and let her collapse.
Love her when she can't get out of bed
because the coming day is just too heavy.
Kiss her cheeks with grace and speak
with lips of kindness.
Her heart is just needing a day to rest.
Love her when it is a good day
and her smile is burning out the sun.
Because it's the only way to love her,
when it's easy and when it's difficult.

-Kayil York
@rose_thorns1921

There are people who see you how you truly see yourself, not like your mirror, neither are they your reflection. They see you through your eyes.

That's how much they love you.
And then there are those who look deeper into you than you ever did, those who recognize your soul, and it becomes both incomprehensibly comforting and utterly terrifying to be around them, for they see both ends on the spectrum of your potential, who you can become, how much you can achieve, and how much you can miss on by not becoming. And you can barely hold your tongue not to ask them for some fortune telling, some tea leaf reading, "Which end of the spectrum am I closer to?"
Then comes Kundera's vertigo crawling its way into your heart, and the desire to fall resonates with you to a shocking degree.
And this in itself is horrifying, that deep inside you, there is this part that craves failure. It lurks right behind the blossoms of your ambition. Then, it either decides to hit hard all at once, or it lingers, feeding on the roots of your dreams, until you forget what your dream has been in the first place.
"Which end of the spectrum am I closer to?" Read your tea leaves, look me in the eye, and tell me I'm closer to becoming.

Tea Leaves

-Basma Eletreby

@basma.etreby

You tell me
I have kind eyes,
and all I know is that
I have never looked at you
without believing
there is permanence
in the world.

-Samantha Gray
@s.l._gray

maybe...I **am** so vain.
maybe after years of being
invisible
...if it makes me vain
for wanting you to look at me
instead of through me.
I see that wistful smile
when you think about your past...
...to want to be that
in your present.
if it makes me vain to want
to be felt so deep that you
need to create me from nothing
I want you to scribble me
on a cocktail napkin
in a bar, with your friends
around and it's so loud but you can't
hear them over the sounds
of composing this thing we are

I want to be the lyric stuck
in your head that wakes you
at 3am, begging to be played
on a dusty guitar in the corner
of your dusty bedroom
I've read you cover to cover
and never once was I a character
in your story
if **that** makes me vain...
I want to be the thing that hurts
you
and the thing that makes the hurt
go away
if that makes me vain...
to be as important to you
as you are
...to want the song to be about
me.

Maybe Carly Simon Was Right
-Isabella Mansfield
@isabellajmansfield

come with me
on a walk through the
garden
of my heart,
let me show you the
beauty
i have been tending to
in the depths of my soul

-Emma lynn
@e.lynn.poetry

If we would live in the same city

Or at least

In the same country

Everything would be alright

We could go to the museum

Once a week

Drink a cup of coffee

When the sun comes out

Red wine at night

Go wandering through the streets of the city

Covered in darkness

If only you would be near

Instead of a thousand miles away

-Pia Rabea Linden

@rabearaphael

I

The simple sight

Of that smile

Has me dreaming,

Thirst-ing

For a touch

Greater than the sensation

Of my two fingers

Sliding inside

Honey.

II

He ran his fingers

On my forearm,

Lingering

At a place

Where I would want

To feel his lips.

III

Put that smile

To good use

And let my flesh

Drown beneath the sharp

Softness

Of your teeth.

-Noemie Del Duca

@ndelducapoetry

And I would study all the physics
To curve space itself
Until distance is warped into nonexistence;
Or perhaps I could create a formula for metamorphosis
So I could become a sparrow and fly
Without worries of borders and planes;
Or perhaps I could engineer a machine
To teleport and transport myself instantly;
Like a mad scientist I dream these theories at night-
What science fiction would allow me
To feel your body sleeping next to mine?

Scientist

-t.s.ink

@inkskratches

Somewhere a man is crawling into bed with a woman he's trying to love but can't because your magnetism is pulling him away like a thirsty hound toward water. He can't explain how he knows but he feels it in his bones.

And somewhere a woman is sitting in a studio apartment in New York that she struggles to afford drinking coffee and sketching out a white dress lined with lace. She is nobody now but in three years her name will be everywhere and her dress will hang in the window of the exact shop you'll walk by with your mother and you will know right away that it's the one.

And somewhere a house is being built by a woman and her wife who will move out in three years' time after their triplets arrive and the little bungalow will be empty at just the right time in just the right place at just the right price.

And though you sleep alone tonight and wonder why things never go your way, just know that your person is coming, the white dress you'll wear when you marry him is being imagined, and the house you'll share until you are old and grey is being built. The universe works in strange and mysterious ways and a life cannot be grown overnight like a tree from magic beans.

But it's magic still, and a magic worth waiting for at that.

Be Patient

-Emily Byrnes

@evergreen.reveries

Lachesis.

Your eyes are tilled soil
deep, rich earth
broken by the budding beets
infantile in existence
with the promise warmth of the sun
After dark afternoons
of gentle Montana rains
cracked by lightning

-Ashley Victoria
@Ashley.victoria.poetry

when you go outside
and collapse into
one of the puddles on the
pavement
left over from the rainstorm
that just shook the world,
take a moment to breathe-
take in the scent of the air,
dig your fingertips deep into
the earth,
listen to the birds coming out
for their next meal,
and appreciate the beauty
for what happens
after the storm

-Emma lynn
@e.lynn.poetry

The Universe lies inside you

All you have to do is see through

You are beautiful in every inch of your skin

And the bizarre thoughts that you think

The way you hold your head high

In the face of a storm

Is as infectious as your enigmatic smile

All your twinkling scars

Add on to your charm

Even when you fought those

Battles unarmed

Break away from the memories

That tore you to pieces

And also made you roar

To that roar

Let that roar

Reverberate with thunder & resilience

Youniverse

-Meghna Shetty

@morosemusings33

The first time I ever saw a miracle
I was only three or four years old
It was a documentary on a girl, a gymnast
Perfect 10's she performed on the beam, vault, and floor-
My mind grew in wonderment at the thought of
Such acrobatic flawlessness
And I dreamed of soaring, dancing, twirling
On the most dangerous of apparatuses-
And when I turned nine
And my mother had some money and time
She took me for a class where I could be
Just like this Romanian goddess I'd seen
But they told me- why she's too old already
And my face grew hot with tears as I cried
For how could my dream have already died?
Then I took a pen in my hand
And wrote the anguishing pain as only a child can
And I realized my hand performed a routine
No different than the gymnast's I'd seen.

Gymnast

-t.s.ink

@inkskratches

I turn my eyes to the heavens
To observe the celestial bodies,
But my eyes were greeted instead
By a panel of grey
On this clouded night.
To myself, I thought,
How unfair that these beauties—
These glorious designs
Of God's own creation—
Are blocked from my sight
By this hideously plain ceiling,
And they cannot do a thing about it!
Oh! But I am no different from the stars above,
Prevented from shining
My light on this world
By those of simpler origin!
Though, I—unlike
My sisters in the sky—
Can push aside this dulling fog
That dares belittle my existence
And suppress my brilliance.
The clouds are but an obstacle
Which shall not deter me
As I strive to shed my radiance
On this world in desperate need
Of illumination.

101.

-c.k.c

@ckayclark

she must be stronger
then they whisper,
for how can a woman
made of glass
walk through wars
and not emerge
with a single scratch?

-Taylor Balfour
@littlesugarwords

I am the moon
as strong as the light
that guides you home
stronger than the stars
in the dark
I am
living
breathing
bold
beautiful
I do not need
your approval
your appreciation
your acceptance
to know
my worth

The Moon
-Aysha Qamar
@aqamar92

He was raised in a fiery home where the emblazoned
craters could swallow you whole; where there were
five to a room; and little Johnny never learned to bloom;
He was raised in a fiery home where the sun's rays
provided the only hug a child ever knew; where there
were no mothers or fathers to sing a requiem for
scarred souls; where the sun serenaded the minds of
little ones with lingering lullabies; with promises
of taking flight in the night sky.
He was raised in a fiery home and learned
to fly too close to the sun; for what did he have to lose
than a momentary home that never taught him to
bloom.

Icarus' Group Home

-Sim Gill

@vv.poetry

on the day i became a woman

my mother cradled me in her arms and said

darling,

only a woman is resilient enough

to bleed out

over

&

over

again

and keep living.

-Elizabeth Anna

@elizabethannapoetry

This is me standing on the edge
Of what's great and what's greater.
I can choose to look back and dwell
In the past
Where guilt and shame
Will
WILL
Surround me
And choke the joy out of my heart,
Or
I could choose to keep walking forward
To take a leap of faith
Into the unknown,
For that is where greater things lie.
Growth lies in the unknown.
No matter where that place leads,
I hope to never look into the past so far that I would continue to live there in my thoughts.
Life is a journey and the ones who don't support you aren't the only ones who are there for you. Life is too short than to do anything less than take care of yourself and love yourself.
So, you do you.
There will always be problems and people who seek to discourage you.
But one thing I have learned is
After you win a battle, there will always be another one.
So ask yourself if you are willing to fight for yourself.
I promise you,
You are worth it.

FIGHT -Esther Marie Gonzales @esther.poetry

She blows smoke
Of the breaths she steals
The only flame
Who has a shadow
The only fire
Who burns when wet

- M. Maan
@mmaanpoetry

some days

i wish nature

would take us back.

take all this blood,

all these bones,

all this ungrateful breath.

climb up our cocky limbs

like ivy,

until we can see the world

only from between

its leafy fingers.

make this mess of us

remember

where we came from.

make us wonder

how

we ever forgot.

reclamation

-Emily May Portillo

@poetry.on.the.exhale

In a paper world
a lead man makes and remakes his life
until he is satisfied
whereas the woman is inked into existence
by a society
trapped in its own traditions...
until now.
Erasable ink allows for greater growth
than ever before.
She can write her own world now;
no longer sentenced to domestic duties,
she can vary her syntax
and play with punctuation.
She is now an editable entity
in charge of her own destiny
and damn anyone who tries to put a full stop
where she wants a comma.

Written in the Cards

-Ron Barton

@teacher2poet

Forgotten memories,
Locked behind the door of my mind,
I run away,
But they find me,
Wrestling me to the ground,
and beating me until I can no longer see,
I'm blinded, broken, fighting my way back,
And with every step I take,
They grab onto my ankles weighing me down with each step,
But I push harder and harder,
Until this time,
I toss them over the edge of insanity,
Watching them torment and scream,
Writhing in non-existence,
There will be nothing left to haunt me again.

The Breakdown

-Shayla B.

@insightfullynaked

my dentist fit me
for a retainer today.

he says I am under stress
and have been clenching my jaw,
pushing my tongue
against my teeth.

I do clench my jaw:
to keep my mouth shut
my tongue bitten and raw
from holding back words
before they pass through
tiny enamel walls
straining with the pressure
and weight of the things
I cannot bear to say.

He says I have to relax
or I may do more damage
to my teeth.
He doesn't know that if I do,
the wrong words may slip
through the spaces between them,
causing damage that
cannot be repaired

It Isn't Stress

-Isabella Mansfield

@isabellajmansfield

Let them laugh

Point to her bare feet

As she climbs mountains

Taller than the sun

-m.a.

@m.a._poetry__

PEOPLE TELL ME THAT I'M CHANGING

I TELL THEM

WHEN SNAKES SHED THEIR SKIN

IT'S CALLED ECDYSIS

THEY SHRED IT

TO ALLOW FOR GROWTH

AND TO REMOVE PARASITES

I NEVER THOUGHT OF MYSELF AS A SNAKE

BUT LOOK

SEE THE SKIN THAT'S LEFT BEHIND

AND I, EMERGING

I, EMERGING

IT'S CALLED ECDYSIS

ECDYSIS

-Olivia Sanders

@poemsbyolivia

I have company over often
But their personalities bring caution
One ridicules everything I do
Whispering under their breath "I hate you"
One doesn't have much to say
Sitting there, emotionless; thoughts astray
One drinks all of my liquor and wine
Stumbling about, assuring everyone "I'm fine"
One checks the lock on the door
One time, two times, three times, four...
I don't know why I ever invite them over
I need to stand my ground, not be a pushover
Mustering the courage to tell them to leave
It's then that I realize, they live inside me

Mental Health Dinner Party

-Kelly Pitt

@blushing_poetry

I'm picking berries

instead of flowers,

because I want colors in mouth.

Colors

(they always

come to me with hunger)

-L.T. Pelle

@l.t.pelle

When the sky pulls you
Away from me
I will not reach for you
Or search the clouds
Hoping to find the Sun—
I will let it rain

Rain

-Kristin Kory

@kristinkory

Mint green memories
Childhood play, crayon-colored walls
Pony tails, chasing sirens, swimming

Aquamarine depths inviting
Treading water, testing limits
Until she can't touch bottom

Turquoise promises glisten
Liquid gold in the sun
Traded Deep-Fried South for Pacific Northwest Wonderland

Sea mist rolls over the Sound
Catlike, lazy wake-up in Emerald City
Illuminates everything she ever wanted

Oh, Little Ocean

-Sarah Herrin

@_SarahHerrin

Pitiful kisses touched by
The neck beneath
Cool palms, in hands
That once danced
Along glass collarbones,

Etched into angry knuckles
Blooming violets on
My tongue in
Sweetness that silenced
The bitten lips between
Your teeth.

Thundered thoughts stain
Tearful veins,
Providing serenity in
Stupidity, to lick
Tasteless dew below
Callus finger-tips
Stroking thigh Over thigh.

The Autumn Index

-Lucy Tasker

@lucyspoetry

tonight i put glitter

on my eyelids

when I looked up

I could see the reflection

of thousands of stars

-Pia Rabea Linden

@rabearaphael

I happened upon a roadside flower
standing tall in the dirt, a bright pink
brighter than other pinks I've seen.
Stopping only for a moment,
I looked on the flower
but I had to move ahead, upon the paved road
because my vehicle rushed to leave.
I wish that I stopped for longer
to admire that flower
to think about the life it lives,
how it breathes fresh air,
grows strong, beautiful, vibrant
and receives from the soil.
Though so many pass it as they drive,
the flower lives a good life by the road,
standing tall in the dirt, a bright pink.

Roadside Flower (About Vietnam)

-Michael Liu

@mikelwords

Everyday I thank the world for the
Hurt it has brought me
For without it, I would not have
Searched deep inside myself
For strength, I would not have
Learned to summon
My own positivity, I would not
Have worked as hard to realize
That pain brings flowers,
For without it I would not have
Grown, sprouted and bloomed.

I Am the Strength Brought By My Pain

-Noemie Del Duca

@ndelducapoetry

You could pull the stars
From the night sky
And still I would stare at it
For they are merely Intricacies
Decorating a vastness
That endless hours would
Still fail to unveil
And so i compare you to the skies
There is no measure
to your complexities

-Sian Marie
@sianmariepoetry

instead of teaching
your daughters
to hide
their femininity
teach your sons
to accept it

we are not
any less
for bleeding
from where
they are given
birth.

Period
-Aysha Qamar
@aqamar92

the wind whistles on beds of irish
as she sucks in her cheeks.
I am merely here,
sitting on her tongue
letting her waves push me
where they please.

-Taylor Balfour
@littlesugarwords

Pressing flowers

pressing news

I was working on a daisy

when they told me of you

Your mind was fragile, reminded

me of the etched glass vase holding

the pink lilies that bloomed despite the frost.

Your body was fragile, reminded

me of how the violet's green stem gives

way under the stronger hand, wilting under

the finger pulling it from the ground.

Flowers and you had so much in common

your beauty and innocence

your fragility

but you can't be pressed the way flowers are,

can't be hidden away in the pages of a book,

a surprise I stumble upon whilst turning yellowed pages

The urgency blossoms

as you're short in span, short in bloom

I'll just have to cherish you before it's too soon

Pressing Flowers

-Olwen Daisy

@olwendaisy_poetry

there is a warmth in this winter
an impermeable joy between
what I say and what I keep silent
buried in murmurs of my bated breath
float paper-white petals of devotion
hands open, you receive all I give,
knowing only you can hold my delight

impermeable joy

-Jenn Dessert

@quiet.little.mercies

A burning mist
of sapphire
sweeps over open mountain peaks
into a valley of milky clouds
that flicker
with electric teeth.
An armada of golden oil-lamps,
burning the dew of endless love,
sails within the airstream
of the breath of God.
Giant trumpets,
blown by colossal angels,
signal our awaited arrival
as a beacon of hope,
beckoning us home
to rest.
I can see,
within the majestic tapestry,
raging sea monsters
reaching through the tempest
as we navigate deathly winds
and turbulent tides—
propelled to safety
by the other side,
beyond the horizon
of infinity's heavenly harbor.

Aeriel

Marc Bayard

@bayard.marc

Outside my window are trees,

Dozens upon dozens of them,

The branches and extensions of each one connected to the others around it,

There are no clear defining lines that determine the complete outline of a single one,

They are all just trees. Plural.

Singularity has lost itself within the forest,

Who can look up and trace every branch, every leaf, every needle, every twig?

The boundaries cease to be realized,

A tangled web of vines, limbs, fruit, and greenery,

They are all.... one.

One single entity amongst the many,

Lost, hiding, trapped,

How can we appreciate the uniqueness and beauty of each one when they are all lumped together?

How can each one thrive to its potential when the taller ones dominate the sun's generosity?

Saplings grow....stunted,

The lushness of its mother has been pruned to twigs and broken limbs,

Distorted and melancholy,

The bark sheds itself from the body,

They are disfigured and succumb to erosion,

And where is the sun to bring sweet relief to their darkness?

The stronger arbors push their way through the tangles,
In the darkness, they push harder and stronger to find the light that brings nourishment,
And so, poking through the tree tops are the broken, neglected pines,
Withered, weathered, worn...
Strategically poking its needles through the canopy,
The sun's rays inject its life, warmth, and energy into it,
Life is being restored to these tattered trees,
These stand taller than the rest and so their uniqueness must be observed by the one looking for it,
Their beauty must be appreciated by those who seek it,
And even though they are intertwined with those that compete to stay alive,
We can see that she is planted firmly in the ground,
She stands out from the rest because we choose to notice her,
We choose to see her,
She is one among the many.

Hardwood Sapling
-Shayla B.
@insightfullynaked

The motherland is calling

Telling me to come home

With the tears that flow the ancestral rivers

Only drinkable by the cups

Of the fluent tongue

But I do not know the motherland

For I am born in a foreign country

That's only survivable by losing

The native roots that have

Desperately been fighting to sprout

Only to be killed off by the

cold white winters

Maybe one day she will forgive me

For not answering her phone calls

Since I am finding roots that are suitable

For these foreign weathers.

The Motherland is Calling

-Beverly Boampong

@b_nhwiren

You are the answer
to a prayer
carried in the bosom
of a whisper
I sent out
to the universe.
I found you
waiting for me
in the dusk
of heartache,
playful and unperturbed,
gesturing me
to plunge
into the wonder
of life.

You led me
to the cusp of love
where twilight,
blistered with
broken dreams,
heals
under compassion's
rosy hues.
Or was it
shades of love
washing over us,
penetrating
this parched skin
that has not known
it's touch.
My tears of joy,
like rain,
slid away
the unkind time
that weighed
upon this
gentle back of mine.

With your hands
you planted love
in this barren soil,
in this place
too rough for the feet
of tenderness to tread.
How was I to know
that one day
you would
bring me here,
where spoken words
are a lackluster thing
when silence clings
to us in awe
of the sight
before our eyes?
Yet
even with such
beauty unfolding
I want nothing more
than to look at you,
because
at the sight of you
every chasm
and peak
that runs
within
my spirit
is illuminated.

In the Bosom of a Whisper
-Harpreet M. Dayal
@harpreet.m.dayal

there is something about houses

that do not have roofs

the way they welcome

rain in without judgment

you have always been a safe place

-Abigail Zerr

@rainbow_ink

we are all beautiful
even if we are lonely
just like the moon.
and even in the darkness
we still shine so bright
from within.
again,
just like the moon.

Lone Moon
-Marsha A.
@poetistpanda

I move my covers away
my last sleeping thought lingers
in my head.
Shane
My kind husband sleeping unrestfully
beside me
As if my dreams were keeping
him from peace.

Finally, I rouse myself to make a cup of tea.
Faces from my past and present
swim up through the brown of mint and honey
in my oversized tea cup
really a soup bowl.
Two a.m. rolls around before I
have calmed my mind enough for sleep.
My side of the bed is cold, so
I snuggle over to my husband,
finally dreaming peacefully.

In the morning he asks me,
"How'd you sleep?"

And I lie.

-Ashley Victoria
@Ashley.victoria.poetry

On hands and knees

Stretched out canvas

Pale wood planks

Strong metal staples

Kaleidoscope of colors

Bold paints in broad strokes

Sparkling splashes of laughter

Happy haphazard patterns

Textures thick and gritty

Full of heart and whimsy

Rainbow of fingerprints

Whole bodies side by side

Ours is no easy task

But we do the work

Breathless and collapsing

Woven fabric ravaged by love

The Lucky Ones

-Sarah Herrin

@_SarahHerrin

When the dust settles

And the sirens become nothing more

Than a distant ringing in your ears

I hope it was worth it—

Losing yourself

While trying to keep them

Where Are You?

-Kristin Kory

@kristinkory

you threw dagger shaped ice cubes

into my fire

pierced so deep

my inferno embers bled

and now the smoke cleared

and you blame me

for our puddle of tears

-Zina Ratinov

@zinaswords

Are you American?
I would be asked as the summer
grew hotter
Where is the flag waving at your
front door?
The colors red, white, and blue on
your shirt?
Where is your pride in the country
that represents your freedom?
I did not understand at that age
that I was expected to fill each page
with an apology for my skin
with an apology for my culture
with an apology for my religion
with an apology for my people
I did not understand at that age
that I was expected to condemn
each act of terrorism
each act of sexism
that was associated with my people
I did not understand at that age
that I was not considered American
that not openly expressing my pride
was taking the wrong side
I will not apologize for my identity
continuously explain to you
that we are the same
despite my name
I am as American as you
and although I often feel
shame
at the decisions our country
has made
it does not make it any less of
mine
as it is yours, realize
America is made on the bricks
of diversity
since the beginning of its time
and that is the truth, not just
some damn line.

American
-Aysha Qamar
@aqamar92

I have spent
most of my life
directing manic mental traffic;
Thoughts supercharged
with vibrant emotional fuel
that have given themselves
the green light
on the highways of my mind.
I have tried to stop them
with roadblocks and red lights,
redirect them into oblivion
but they return with momentum,
surpassing the speed limit with ease.
I wonder if they will one day learn
how to break the sound barrier
with their incessant noise
and cause an explosive clash
and if I will be a simple observer
or their helpless victim,
stuck in the wreckage.

Collision Course

-Marc Bayard

@bayard.marc

I've drifted for years on unstirred waters
too far into the sea
away from the warmth of home
I've folded and stored my sails
certain that my face
would never feel the wind again

But now an easy breeze is kissing my cheek
refreshingly cool and steady
unexpectedly exciting the waters
With hope I will raise my sails
as arms unto the sun
praying this new breeze might guide me home

New Breeze
-Michael Liu
@mikelwords

Flowers are the perfume of heaven
my mother whispers, grasping my small
hands, tucking my hair under my ear.
They line the streets up there, petals
adorning the gold pavement
Flowers are medicine for every illness
my mother says to me as we cut and dry
a few, a get-well-soon for one in need of care.
She speaks of yellow roses, the ones that
lined her grandmother's room, sweetening
the air and how their yellow seemed to have
a smell itself, one that escaped the flower
and went straight to her mouth, curling it up
in a wide grin
So, listen close, because you'll meet a few
a few who need a little tender loving
and when you do
remember my words and that in heaven
flowers are the perfume of old

Perfume of Heaven

-Olwen Daisy

@olwendaisy_poetry

Atropos.

This cannot be the end
because people
are not just bodies,
not just limbs,
not just bones and tissue and skin,
not a collection of cells,
not just a sequence of genes.

Because the heart
is not just a drum
that beats out the tune of a life.

Because a life
is not just the body
that contains it
this time around.

And the soul
barely even notices these things
as it passes through,
as it crosses our paths,
brief lifetimes,
with a nod.

But we notice.
Those of us still contained
within these bodies,
still defined
by our genes

and our words
and our deeds,
still tethered to our paths
by hearts that beat.
We notice when you pass.

But regardless, regardless –
and no matter what box they put you in –
this cannot be the end.

Because I still have words
to describe you.
Because we are all of us magicians
and we can conjure people up
in our hearts.
Because you defined me, in part,
with your part in my life.
Because a life
is what you make of it
and I will make yours last,
with my words
and my deeds
and my heart,
with a nod
towards wherever you are,
until our paths cross again.

This Cannot Be the End

- Daphne Kapsali

@dkapsali

i was Samson once

the powers of youth

the world my preemptive playground

the possibilities endless

but you anesthetized

my spirit into slumber

with your heavenly promises

then shaved my head

with long cold sheers

my prisoner eyes

under a bald head stared back at me

through the tear drenched mirror

they didn't tell

that Samson was a woman

that hair grows back

longer, mightier

stronger than her virgin youth

for what I lacked in strength

I now make up

in strands of courage

those locks now

fly untamable

in the free wind

do i need to be Samson

to be a warrior?

Samson (Dedicated to Hasidic Child Brides)

-Zina Ratinov

@zinaswords

she seemed like a shooting star
always providing light & hope to others
but keeps falling, keeps breaking, keeps burning
on her own...

— S A E H
@bysaeh

You don't hum anymore.
I remember you skipping 'round the kitchen
in cotton shorts
making cocoa,
pretending it was coffee
humming lullabies the moon taught you
talking about how you couldn't wait till nine months pass
talking about painting the spare room elephant-grey
so he or she could decide on their own who they wanted to be
telling me they would grow up and fix the world;
you could feel it.
You'd put my hand on your belly
and even though it was too early for kicks
it was fun to pretend.
Spring came and Summer
but never the kicks
and nine months came and went
and it's just you and me in the kitchen
drinking caffeinated anything and lots of wine
and the elephant-grey room is full of boxes and old guitars and invisible
sadness
-so much sadness-
and you don't hum

anymore.

You Don't Hum Anymore
-Emily Byrnes
@evergreen.reveries

She was made of paper
Of fragile old books
Of stories of other people
That other people had told
So when her binding broke
Everything began to unfold
Her body fluttered apart
Pages taking flight in the wind
And when they were gone
Nothing was left but
The spine of a skeleton

Made Up of Stories
-Ryan Pirtle
@bi_literary

To write, one simply cannot
wear their heart upon a sleeve.
One must RIP it from their
chest, beating, bleeding, exposed
for the world to see.

-Anne Joseph
@_annie_jo_

Depression is a lot like dying.
You breathe.
Exist.
Blink.
Repeat.
A zombie of sorts.
Feeding off of others.
Selfishly trying to live,
While dying.
Breathing. Existing. Blinking.
Repeat.
And if you're lucky,
It lets you live again.

Live Again
-Kelly Pitt
@blushing_poetry

I watch the man at the bus stop
Pull from his cigarette
Like it is the only
Breath he has taken all day

I wonder if it is.

I wonder
If when we let the things we love
Tear at our lungs
Long enough
They become the only thing
Beaten organs can breathe

that boy burned me
he was my two packs a day
since '75 or maybe sooner
-Ally Gundrum
@thatonepoetrygirl

I'm not enough

I know,

so let me go.

It hurts to be

half loved.

-Perry Poetry

@perrypoetry

i leapt with joy
fins and tail followed suit
enthralled to explore your world

but imagination
was the short end
being caught in your reel

when i curl my lip up
it still bleeds
at the site where your hook cut deep

your kisses sting me now
my little fish mouth
suckling bubbles of pained joy

your oxygen was not my lifeline
now i swim in my own waters again
an ocean of possibilities

i am very much still alive
hook line and sinker; not yours

they say there are plenty of fish
-Zina Ratinov
@zinaswords

Dear Anxiety,

Go take a walk once in a while
Enjoy the view on the ferris wheel
Get lost in the middle of a busy street
Shape shift through cities and sleepless nights
Bungee jump through deadlines

Abandon your precious home
For your presence
Affects my well-being
Breathless hours & vicious unproductivity
Constantly reminds
Of what I can't be

Dear Anxiety
-Meghna Shetty
@morosemusings33

a beast reins over me, weakens
me, breaks me, tears me apart.
shakes me, abuses me, arrests my
heart.
strips my clothes, body and
honour,
never stopping for the next
two hours.

lifeless, i lie on his bed
crying, screaming
but not a tear is shed.
he violates my purchased body,
marks his territory,
and when he is done,
i'm tossed back to my owner,
who takes me, displays me,
gives me a price.

they look at me; my face,
body and beauty, wondering
my worth, a hundred
pounds or rupees.

they come from all over
to have me on lease,
a day, a month, an hour
is how long they may keep
and when they are done,
i am tossed back to my owner,
who gives me a title, not worthy
of honour.

my body and soul never meet.
i am only a woman,
a woman without a face.
a woman in a trade,
and even when i have died
a thousand times,
they take me, sell me, and recycle
me
some more.

Without a Face
-Sim Gill
@vv.poetry

The spell broke just as quickly as our eyes met; half dazed, it was your enigmatic smile that roped me in, promising the world beneath desolate words, tongue ivy spiked.
And yet, my maiden heart, naive in her hope, fell deeply, madly, infinitely into the cauldron of your empty promises, brimming with betrayal, heartache, aeons of pain.
And although I lay sinking beneath bubbling resentment, I grabbed hold of the edge, of my worth, propping me above the toxic waste of your half hearted love.
Hair dripping wet with memories left barren and cold, I rose from the cauldron, the ashes left burning beneath my broken heart still smouldering in their pain.
But I was no longer a prisoner of your caged love; no longer privy to the ghost you carved out of my soul; free of the cords you so neatly, so meticulously tied to my being, nestled deep within the crimson crevices of my beating heart.
The witch you tried to burn in your wake no longer cast under your spell.
I was free; to be the wild woman I longed to be.
The wild hearted soul my great grandmothers grandmothers fought for me to be.
And I won't let them down.
I won't let myself down.

Liberata Elevatum
-Tina Pitropakis
@tp.poetess

You are a dangerous human being
to a soul like mine
you are destructive
and only love
when you feel like it
because you run from yourself
down bottles and dollar
bills rolled up tight and you
don't ever listen
to a goddamn thing I try to pull
you back up but every time I turn
my back you jump back in
and so many times I have yelled
and I have screamed
and pleaded and cried but you,
are a creature of habit
and I,
do want these things
I want more

-Linnea m.d.
@linnea_m.d

At least I got to have
the treasure of our memories
I open it once in a while to know how fortunate I am
to have you once in my life
& with all these, I'll be the richest I've ever been

- S A E H
@bysaeh

Laying with lilies
In a field plagued with deception
The petals, no recollection
Of who they were before they withered
Withered, wavering under the abyss of death's climax
Plush petals nothing but a distant memory
Trying to exist being their only felony
In a world that no longer cared for the tender
They could no longer withstand being a defender
Of themselves.

Laying with lilies
The girl lays aimlessly staring into the nothingness of the world
Lilies whispering hymns of death's past
Tattered voices of others that had laid where she lays
She feels herself start to slowly fray
The sad part, it's the most alive she'd felt all day
As the bitter sweet nectar of nothingness
Tantalizes and erupts on her buds
She gives in, sending a mental message to all of whom she loves
For the lily's whisper promises of life that is above
She gives in because with life, she's had enough

They engulf her, gnawing on all signs of life

Rejuvenating themselves

Whaling and praying it will bring them back to life

So that they could be again

Feed again

Their colour returns

Her body burns as it disintegrates

The lilies stand tall

For they'd won

Replenished themselves, ready for the next body to come.

The girl's no longer laying with the lilies

Instead, amongst the field of many that had given in before.

Her neighbour whispering 'Welcome to the field of deception'

Lilies

By Molisha Madison

@molishas.mind

Under the swell of my breast,

My heart is breaking loudly,

Drowning out the sound of you taking a chainsaw to my smile,

I watch you leave me, holding the dismembered remnants of our life,

I watch you toss aside my heart,

It was useless to you anyhow,

I'm in too many pieces and missing the edges,

Who will solve my puzzle now?

Horror Movie Love

-Bettie Schade

@bettie_schade

She has a dancer living underneath her skin. She twirls and crawls but does not appear to touch the ground. She has a serpentine shadow crawling within. All dressed in black, the outline of her figure is barely visible. With grace and malice, she lures you in, not driven by an interest in you, but in finding an exit for herself, a way out. With every whimsical move she makes, she hopes to stretch that skin, render it a bit looser, freer, her own.

She fights to make space for herself there too, underneath skin that has been a little too tight. But when she finds she's fought back, forced to submit, she yields, but with her she takes away your joy and awe. She leaves you plain, too plain to be told apart from anyone else. She crawls back into her tiny nook in your imagination. And you think you win. You have a dancer dying underneath your skin.

Dancer

-Basma Eletreby

@basma.etreby

trauma

builds muscles

we never knew we had.

-Elizabeth Anna

@elizabethannapoetry

One, two, three.

I count my eggs and put them in your basket

but your hands are careless

they cannot hold it steady

so they crack

(one, two, three)

Yellow yolk oozes through the woven belly of the basket.

And you want me to give you my heart?

Please.

You can't even keep groceries safe.

Counting Chickens

-Emily Byrnes

@evergreen.reveries

I talked to the moon,
Seven confessed sin,
For duty's Ripe slits
In favour of punctured Skin.

I told the moon,
I watched him grin,
Sipping tears of
Grey palms,
Promised, through thick
And thin.

I spoke to the moon,
He commanded I begin,
Tasting body's sweetest
Dew, hooked on human
Heroin.

Letters to the Moon
-Lucy Tasker
@lucyspoetry

and so

the girl

who could get high

off of words

had run out of them.

and instead

was simply

engulfed

by pure

sadness.

the pit in her stomach

had turned into

the throb

of her heart.

not because someone had broken it

but because she had hurt herself.

because self disappointment

and admitting

that she

was being the person

she tried so hard

not to be

hurt more

than anything anyone else

could have done

to her.

guilty

-Grace

@fairly.grace

Boys who break hearts
Should not stand around corners
That I walk in the mornings

Should not play guitars
With fingers I held
In guidance
Before he knew the notes

Boys who shatter spines
And collapse throats

Should not tell me I'm beautiful
(Don't fucking cry to me right now)
Tell me I'm perfect
(I will never trust you)
Tell me I'm wanted
(Don't smile at him)
Tell me I am loved
(Go fucking cry to him)

Boys who build cages
Shouldn't teach me how to love

They should just
Leave

-Ally Gundrum
@thatonepoetrygirl

You speak to me every half a second
Between the tics and tocs
Somehow I feel haunted
You've left a printed soul of you in me
I sense your existence with every blink
I relive our moments with light speed
Even my dreams, are burnt films
Nothing is left but tiny clips
Of your bright screaming eyes
The things they behold are so quiet
Am tired of thinking of you,
Am tired of not hearing you,
I miss you..

-Adem Osman
@acrookedpoet

i have known so many people
with shovels for hands.
you are not the first.
so, please, do not be ashamed.
i know you cannot help yourself.
and i know i cannot stop you
once you begin to dig a hole.
dig a ditch.
dig a grave.
dig a tunnel
into the depths of despair.
dig yourself deeper
and deeper
until disaster
has made a home out of you.
but, trust
that on the days
when you do not have the strength
to dig yourself
out,
i will come.

i will come
devoted and determined.
with white knuckles
and dirt-caked fingernails.
i will dig
to bring you back
from the darkness.
because some days
my hands
look a lot like shovels, too.
some days
i find dirt in my ears
and a pounding in my skull.
some days,
when i am neck deep and desperate for air,
i find that my arms
are suddenly more earthworm than pickaxe.
all the muscle dissolved into ache.
some days,
all i can hope for
is someone to haul me out.

so when i say,
i understand,
what i mean to say is,
i know well the way sorrow
can taste like soil on the tongue.
the way it can slide gritty down the throat.
settle like a graveyard in the chest.

when i say
i am not afraid
to get my hands dirty,
what i mean to say is,
i love you.
what i mean to say is,
i will not let you
be buried alive.

dig

-Emily May Portillo

@poetry.on.the.exhale

softer & softer

grief circles back

there will come a day

when its arrival

is no longer the startle

of bird into glass

it learns to land

with wings as delicate

as breath

it learns to sing

a celebration of those

lost to death

on grief

-Scott-Patrick Mitchell

@spmpoet

Something about your
darkness seemed to
match mine
And the world and the
sadness became lighter
over time

-JCM
@jcm.poems

I am the child

Of the dying sun

And the fearful night

The horizon is a home to me

I know nothing but division

-m.a.

@m.a._poetry__

Snow, white

bone weeping,

my head makes my teeth ache

-L.T. Pelle

@l.t.pelle

I have learned the value of breaking down.
I mean when I tell you that while it hurts,
it is also healing.
Scattering your pieces out
and gluing them back together
will be a repeated process.
But it will also make you realize
the beauty of becoming brand new.
Over and over and over again.

-Kayil York
@rose_thorns1921

she was always
caught in the dance
of what she was
and what she was to be,
and there she stood,
paralyzed in the middle,
not quite
becoming either.

-Taylor Balfour
@littlesugarwords

A seven-headed serpent lies in wait,
For one so great,
white knight to face
my demons for me,
Enter the gates,
And try to save me for,
A reason never spoken of,
My demons hunger, "more"
Sharpened sword and a hero's ego,
Save the princess
and the day,
I am my demons,
the seven-headed snake
that lied in wait,
in this
my hellscape,
and you,
you look like dinner.

Beware

-Bettie Schade

@bettie_schade

I asked the question with a loaded gun, "How are you?".
You looked at me like I was holding you for ransom; a hostage situation I didn't know I was a part of.
I hovered back, hand still gripping the rifle I'd somehow come to hold.
I looked beyond your gaze, and then I saw him.
The boy you once were; frightened, cowering in the corner of the room; lost in a world he'd tried so hard to find his place in.
I surrendered my weapon to the floor, laying it to rest at my feet, and approached you with care.
I put my arm around you as a show of support, and watched as your tears flooded the carpet beneath us.
And as we sat there, the water rising with every shrieking cry, the tears that made rivers along your cheeks and oceans at your feet began to lift you, allowing you to float and feel free.
In that moment, freedom was yours.
Exonerated by your tears, you surrendered to yourself.
And as you drifted off out of sight, the flood before us cleared, leaving but a man holding a rifle in one hand and bullets in the other.
You had saved yourself from the kidnapping that had caged you in the confines of your mind for years.
Disarming your old beliefs and releasing yourself to the world once more.
You were finally free.
You were finally free to be all you could be.
You were finally free to be yourself.

Freedom

-Tina Pitropakis

@tp.poetess

What your problem is?

You keep picking up sunflowers

And expect them to be roses

Two beautiful flowers with

Different petals

I'm Not Her

-Beverly Boampong

@b_nhwiren

HOW FRIGHTENING IT WAS

TO REALIZE

BEAUTIFUL BOY

YOU HAVE NO SOUL

AND THOSE OCEAN EYES

I THOUGHT TOLD STORIES

OF PAIN AND TRUTH AND LOVE

ARE MERELY SHALLOW POOLS

STAGNANT AND DECEPTIVE

I AM THE ONE

WHO HOLDS THE SEA

AND NOW I UNDERSTAND

FOOLISH GIRL

I FELL IN LOVE

WITH MY REFLECTION

Reflection

-Olivia Sanders

@poemsbyolivia

I'm sorry, I had to go away for a while there—

that's what it feels like in my head

one half, trying to kiss the other

one piece is bright yellows oranges pinks

but the other is dark

and cold,

and they do their best to coexist

inside my imagination using

fire and flowers

to create whatever I am

but when I start to lose my balance

everything begins to swirl

I forget how to eat

and so I don't

and I forget how to walk

so I lay in bed

and I cannot remember how to use my words

and so I spit out whatever I can find

my mind slips on how to care

and so I watch myself bleed

the fire in me

cannot be left alone

as it will destroy

its own home

until the flowers grow back

-Linnea m.d.

@linnea_m.d

your fingertips of
whiskey and bonfire
spread sparks of
revolution across my skin.
in the taste of war and
warmth of other sins,
I feel the chaos in my exhale.
I scream.
I am not made for this.
You smile, then whisper,
Burn, love, burn.

whiskey and bonfire
-Jenn Dessert
@quiet.little.mercies

He thinks

If he flies into the sun

Open eyes

Open heart

He will feel bright again

So he tries to outstare

Sunlight

Forgetting that

Like the hell he left

His sun is flame

So I sit in the riverbed

Watching him scorch his hands

As he flies into the sun

Open heart

Open eyes

Telling himself as his vision

Fades

Love is blind

Love is blind

Love is blind

Icarus' Fallacy

-Ally Gundrum

@thatonepoetrygirl

My anxiety never leaves
It's like a ghostly beast that no one ever sees
Always there and always sniffing for meat

Depression stops by regularly to comment on
the state of my house
and the deep imprint of my body in my bed

Mania is that friend I always get into trouble with
Pouring wine down my throat and keeping me awake
Convincing me to do reckless things

Mixed is a set of twins who invite themselves over
One maxes out my cards and throws away my meds
While the other replays his homemade documentary on what
a horrible person I am

Stability is an old friend I rarely see
But when I do, it's precious time
She reminds me that these characters are not me

Meet the Cast of Characters
-Ryan Pirtle
@bi_literary

I blossom beautifully

without you here

You were all thunder

and no rain.

-JCM

@jcm.poems

It's not that I talk too much
It's that I say too much
I wait until the words build up
And drop like acid from my tongue
I've killed relationships this way
Walked right up and gave them the kiss of death
When I thought I was just showing love

It's not that I don't talk enough
It's that I don't say enough
I don't know when to be guarded and when to be vulnerable
I often switch them up, play one when I should be the other
Filling my real relationships with fluff
Feeding bad relationships with my weaknesses

Because I'd rather be kicked when I'm down
I'd rather not hear the good things you have to say
It creates a literal tension in my body, I curl into myself like I was punched in the gut
I know, some have felt that tension emanating off of me
I'm that transparent in my hate

I don't know how to want good things for myself

Gut Punch
-Ryan Pirtle
@bi_literary

When these fragile bones

Wash ashore

And find you

Piled up and broken

Lifeless, but not dead

I want you to know—

This is not the end

Not the End

-Kristin Kory

@kristinkory

ACKNOWLEDGMENTS

To all of the poets who contributed to this anthology: Emma, Saeh, Meghna, Isabella, Emily B., Annie, Noemie, Scott-Patrick, Taylor, Esther, Munroop, Connie, L.T., Daphne, M.A., Jenn, Sim, Bettie, Ryan, Sarah, Elizabeth, Kelly, Abigail, Jesselyne, Allison, Aysha, Marsha, Linnea, Sian, Olivia, Ron, Zina, JCM, Marc, Beverly, Shayla, Ashley, Ghabiba, Tanu, Lucy, Kristin, Perry, Molisha, Basma, Grace, Olwen, Adem, Pia, Michael, Tina, Emily P., Kayil, Harpreet, Leah, & Samantha. Never stop writing.

To Sean Cairns, for creating such a beautiful painting for the cover. To Brady Wolchansky, for designing the cover and working hard to make sure I made my deadline. To Will Evans for giving me the courage I needed to pursue the dream of starting my publishing company. To Shane, my wise and passionate companion.

To the thousands of poets who submitted to be a part of this anthology and were not chosen: keep submitting and keep creating; Augie's Bookshelf will continue the journey of publishing these anthologies.

Thank you.

Molly Wolchansky, founder of Augie's Bookshelf

@augiesbookshelf on Instagram

Made in the USA
Coppell, TX
06 October 2020